Marshmallow Toes

By Melissa Clemens

Illustrations by
Floyd Ryan Yamyamin

AuthorHouse™
1663 Liberty Drive
Bloomington, IN 47403
www.authorhouse.com
Phone: 1-800-839-8640

Published by AuthorHouse 02/19/2013

ISBN: 978-1-4817-1135-7 (sc)
*   978-1-4817-1154-8 (e)*

Library of Congress Control Number: 2013901682

authorHOUSE®

Cameron never cleaned between his toes. He absolutely refused to do it!

"I'm NOT cleaning between my toes! I like the SQUISH SQUISHEE SQUISH of the toe jam I keep between them!" he yelled.

"Cameron," his mother said with a sigh, "you must clean your toes, it isn't healthy to leave that gunk between them!"

"Why?" He said, "I don't brush my teeth with them, I don't comb my hair with them! I don't even eat with them! I only cover them up with socks when I put on my shoes!

"If you don't take care of your toes, bad things will happen. It's bath time, up the stairs sir!"

Cameron climbed into the bathtub with his glowing green rubber frog Frank. Frank's eyes never closed so Cameron always used him as a witness for bath time. "No Mommies in the bathroom please!" Cameron yelled.

Cameron scrubbed his hair, his ears, and his face. He washed under his arms, behind his knees and everywhere in between. He even washed his belly button twice. But he absolutely would not under any circumstances wash between his toes. He even propped his feet up on the edge of the tub so he could admire his toe jam collection. His toes had a slight brownish green cast between them and an aroma that was less than sweet. Cameron didn't care.

Cameron climbed out the tub and dried off. He slipped into his favorite pj's and Mom came up to tuck him in.

"Okay, time for inspection! Hair.....ears.....face.....very nice. Under your arms..... behind your knees.....smells sweet....but what's that smell...uh....YUCK! Cameron you didn't clean your toes!" She yelled.

"I told you I won't. I like my toe jam. Sorry Mom." He said with a grin.

"Well, I guess you will have to learn the hard way. Good night Darling, remember I warned you. Mom kissed him and turned out the light.

Cameron sat straight up the next morning and looked around the room. His train set was still on the floor. His closet door was still closed. His lucky pen was still on his desk.

He jumped out of bed with both feet and was about to slide his feet into his slippers when he looked down and screamed,

"AAAAAAHHHHHHHH!!! MY TOES!!!!!"

Where each of his ten toes had been there were now ten marshmallows! He ran down the hall and slid down the banister into the kitchen. Dad was sitting at the table drinking his orange juice.

"Dad!" he yelled. "My toes are missing!"

His dad chucked without looking up.

Cameron didn't wait for an answer. He hopped out the door to the Sun room where Mom was doing her yoga.

"MOM!" He screamed! "MY TOES! THEY ARE MARSHMALLOWS! HELP!"

"Oh dear," his mother said. "Now how are you going to take care of your toes? I warned you. It's done now. Today is Saturday we have to go to the town picnic. Go and get ready, you will have to wear your flip flops I guess."

Cameron stepped carefully back up the stairs with his feet spread wide. "I won't be showing off my toes in flip flops," he said. "I know just the thing."

He tried to put on his tennis shoes but couldn't fit all five marshmallows under the tongue.

He tried his hiking boots but as soon as they were laced he could feel the marshmallows melting and feeling gooey from the heat.

He decided to just cover them with his socks and hope nobody noticed but his feet looked so big, it looked like he had a bar of soap stuck into each sock.

"It's hopeless," he said dismally. "All of my friends are going to call me a freak!"

Cameron slipped on his flip flops and went to sit on his swing in the backyard to wait. He was very sad. So sad he didn't even swing.

He just sat there staring at his ridiculous marshmallow toes.

"Maybe it's not so bad," he thought. "Nobody else will have them. I'll call them a fashion statement."

Just as he started to cheer up he noticed a trail of ants marching towards his marshmallow toes.

"Aahhhhh!!!" He yelled. He shimmied up the homemade ladder that went to his tree house and sat on the landing hugging his knees.

"If the ants eat my toes I'm doomed!" he huffed breathlessly. He reached in and grabbed a bottle of water he had left here yesterday. When the ants started up the tree, he poured the water on them in a gush.

They lost interest and marched away.

"Phew! That was close." He sighed.

As he sat feeling sorry for himself about the ants, he spotted two squirrels barking at each other two branches up. They had their heads together barking quietly and pointing at Cameron's toes.

Very slowly the bigger one started climbing down the tree licking his lips.

"AaahhhH!" Cameron yelled.

"Aaaahhhh!" the squirrel barked back, but he kept creeping down.

With the ants prowling below and the squirrel above, Cameron had no choice.

Cameron jumped onto the doghouse below and grabbed the hook that held the birdfeeder. He swung around it to the ground.

He was giggling excitedly.

He was almost having a good time until he looked down at his marshmallow toes.

They were covered in birdseed!

"How do you clean marshmallow?" He wondered.

All at once a flock of blackbirds landed on the power line above. They squawked at him,

"CAKE, CAKE, CAKE!

"It's not cake! It's my toes! He screamed at the birds. They started landing one by one on the ground around him.

"AAAAhhhhhh!" he yelled loudly and ran for the house.

When he got to the house he was breathless. He ran inside and slammed the door. He was breathing hard when his mother found him.

"Cameron are you okay? Are you ready to go to the picnic?" she asked.

"I can NOT go to the picnic Mom. My marshmallow toes barely survived the backyard!" he exclaimed with panic. "I will clean between my toes from now on! I will have the cleanest toes in the neighborhood!"

"If you are sure you will clean between your toes I will help you. Do you promise? " She asked.

"I promise! Please Mom!" he cried.

"Okay go have a seat on Dad's chair and cover your eyes."

When Cameron's eyes were covered, Mom crept back into the living room and pulled the marshmallows off his toes. She crept back out quietly.

When she came back she said "Okay Cameron," Open your eyes!"

"Oh Mom! Thank you, thank you! I will go wash my toes right this minute. I will never collect more than one days toe jam ever again!" He promised.

"Okay, son," she said. "Now go scrub your toes and get dressed for the picnic."

And that's exactly what he did.

THE END.

CPSIA information can be obtained at www.ICGtesting.com
Printed in the USA
BVIW12n0612191015
422788BV00002B/2